I love you, Mummy

This book belongs to

_____

_____

Written by Jillian Harker
Illustrated by Kristina Stephenson

This edition published by Parragon in 2011

Parragon
Queen Street House
4 Queen Street
Bath BA1 1HE, UK

Copyright © Parragon Books Ltd 2004

ISBN 978-1-4454-5414-6

Printed in China

I love you, Mummy

Bath · New York · Singapore · Hong Kong · Cologne · Delhi
Melbourne · Amsterdam · Johannesburg · Auckland · Shenzhen

"Watch me, Mummy," called Little Bear. "I'm going fishing."

"Wait a minute," replied Mummy Bear. "There's something you might like to know."

But Little Bear was already
running down to the river.

Mummy Bear ran too.

She saw Little Bear
jump onto a rock.

She saw Little Bear
reach out his paw
to catch a fish.

Then Little Bear began to teeter and totter.

"This doesn't feel so good!" thought Little Bear.

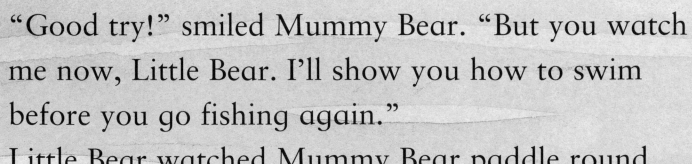

"Good try!" smiled Mummy Bear. "But you watch me now, Little Bear. I'll show you how to swim before you go fishing again."

Little Bear watched Mummy Bear paddle round and round.

"Your turn now, Little Bear," she said.

Little Bear did exactly what Mummy Bear had done. "This feels good!" thought Little Bear. "I love Mummy."

"Look at me, Mummy," called Little Bear. "I'm going to pick those fruits."

"Just a minute," replied Mummy Bear. "There's something you might like to know."

But Little Bear was already climbing the tree.

Mummy Bear saw
Little Bear run
along a branch.

She saw Little Bear
reach out his paw to
pick a juicy fruit.

Then Little Bear began to wibble and wobble.

CRASH!

"This doesn't feel like fun!" thought Little Bear.

"Not bad!" said
Mummy Bear. "But
you look at me now,
Little Bear. I'll show you
how to climb properly
before you go fruit-picking
again."

Little Bear watched
how Mummy Bear
balanced as she
climbed.
"Your turn now, Little
Bear," she said.

Little Bear did what Mummy Bear had done.
"This tastes good!" thought Little Bear.
"I love Mummy."

"Look, Mummy," smiled Little Bear. "All the other cubs are playing. I'm going to play, too."
"Wait a minute, please," said Mummy Bear.
"There's something you might like to know."

Little Bear stopped and turned. "Tell me," he said.
"Be gentle when you play," said Mummy Bear.
"Look. Like this." Mummy Bear reached out her paws.
She wrapped her arms round Little Bear. She rolled
Little Bear over and over on the ground.

"I love Mummy," thought Little Bear. Then he ran off to play. He did just what Mummy Bear had done.

And it felt like

fun!

Mummy Bear kissed Little Bear's sleepy head.

"I love you, too," she said.

"Goodnight, Little Bear."